A little background about how
this came about;
During lockdown, a year ago, I started to
write poetry and short stories,
firstly about the Coronavirus and then
ending with my nature poems.
Hoping to make friends smile...
and they did.

Acknowledgements

I would like to say a warm thank you, Sam and Frances for my beautiful book cover.

A special thank you to Heather, for my sending her a poem most days and her continued encouragement.

Warmest thoughts to Lynne for doing the same, to all my friends and family for their support in such hard ever changing times, for all of us.

I set to write a collection of poems about how I felt, love and my love of nature during the last ten months. After being chosen for

an entry to the Hailsham Festival 2020 Anthology, this gave me the boost I needed.
I have been writing poems since 1995 and include the published My Dance and Teen Girl Blues from the following year, the rest have never been published.

A small donation from hopeful sales will go to the local food bank and Hailsham 95.9 FM which have also given me great support with my poems and stories.

Coronavirus Days

Coronavirus Days

Food boxes and no loo rolls,
Isolation and it's taking it's toll!
Clapping at the window or door
Missing family more and more.
Choirs and meet up all on zoom
I wouldn't be surprised if there's a 'baby boom'
Loving our gardens and the birds
Local radio playing with song words.
Our heart will finally leap
As we hug our families and weep …
For the virus has almost gone
It's time to laugh and have a sing song.

Published in The Hailsham Festival Anthology 2020.

Mum's Thank-you

When the chips were down

Oh, how you rallied around.

Such kindness to so many -

Sons, Daughters, Sisters even Uncle Kenny.

Ordering the shopping for Mum,

With basics, but secretly popping in a bun!

For the many weeks ahead

We stayed in our houses before going to bed.

Gardens became a 'magical' place to sit,

And watch the flowers and the odd Blue Tit.

Until we were told we could go out

And visit you all again and get about.

So, it's a thank-you from us all,

For shielding us behind a safe wall.

Sunday in June.

What are you doing this Sunday in June,
What are you doing this afternoon?
We can go out together and sit in the sun,
Or just sit together and share a bun.
Then jump and shout,
Or be happy to run about.
As this we pray, will all be over,
This scary thing that they call Covid.

Go to your room

Go to your room, I was told,
As a child it felt very cold!
At first the guilt for what was done,
Staring out of the window was no fun.
Now many years have passed,
I find myself home, where I last -
Had feelings of being alone.
Now my 'room' has grown to four,
Life has become such a 'bore',
To wake and feel a pounding chest,
As I sit on my bed, put to the test!
Of what is going on outside -
For a blanket of virus, has spread around,
You can not see it on the ground…
It's jumping from one and all,
So you have to hide behind walls!
Once you are out and free,
It knocks you to your knees.
But now we will fight back -
With a vaccine to attack…
To once again feel safe,
And be able to leave this place.

Various

Teen Girl Blues

So what if I want to dye my hair yellow
And go out with every passing fellow.
No I won't tidy my room
I wouldn't know how to use a broom!
Yes, I like my TV on until 12 o'clock
And don't you forget if you enter my room to, KNOCK!
My make-up is mainly in black…
but does not look like I have just risen from the sack.
But really, I do still like a sympathetic ear
And it's good to know Mum, you're always here
Every time I shed a tear. ♥

Found to be.

I started to cut a banana,
And then a sultana,
Into a coffee, I had made!
There was nothing to do,
But to stop this ballyhoo,
And rest for a while…
Until I looked at my dial,
Raised my sleepy head,
Quickly jumped from my bed -
Was it a dream!
All is not as it seems.

My Grandsons

My Grandsons are very on the ball
And both are getting very tall.
They ask if Nanny was around when Dinosaurs walked
They read their stories and talked -
About the day I came to stay
We laughed as we watched 'Woody', in the hay
And the Parrot, that could mime
We really did have a good time…
Until I have to go and I miss them 'so'
Because we share a bond tied tight as a bow.
But it won't be long till I come again
And we dance away, now let's work out when? ♥♥

Lost my glasses, Again!

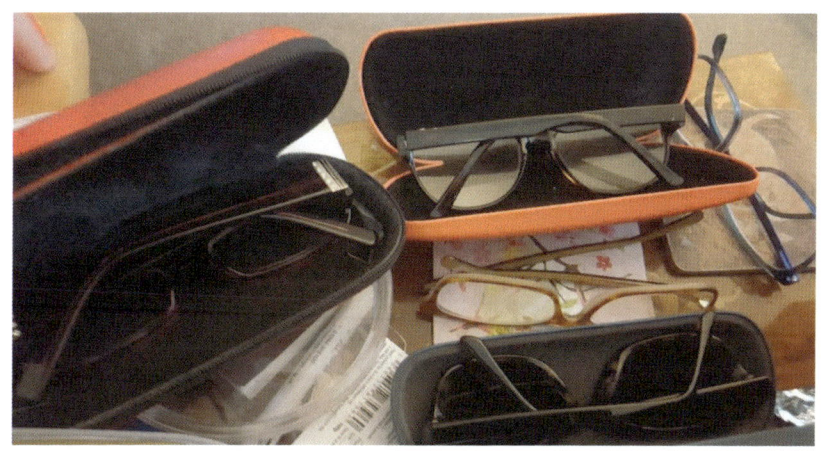

'Yes,' I feel it's a common tale,
But more for female than male.
Unless, I tie my glasses around my neck,
They disappear and I can not see a speck!
Are they down my sofa,
Or maybe in Ted's loafer? ☺
No, it seems I need to think back,
To get on the right track-
I hope not in the rubbish sack!
Are they in my latest bag,
Or under the gardening mag?
No! it's just as my pets are being fed,
I find they are sitting on my 'head'.

My Great Friend.

The Church bells rang,
And the blackbirds sang,
The day you came to stay..
My great friend, it's like you have never been away!
Fellow lover of birds and bees,
And delicious, Sunday cream teas.
You knew my secrets very well,
But you would never kiss and tell.
So I am glad you are passing this way,
Even for a night and day.

My Fluffy Comfort Rug

He comes and lays by me, a fluffy comfort rug,

It is in his eyes as he looks up at me, he knows I am sad.

I stroke his thick cream fur and stop the sadness,

The knowing he will always be faithful to me, unconditionally!

Unlike the person who has changed their mind…

About if I was right for their tight fit lifestyle.

Pets will always be there for you.

Be kind to them and remember the love they give you.

All they want is a stroke and some food -

They don't ask for much, but you are their world ♥

The Soldier Stood Alone

The soldier stood alone, standing tall and proud,
Standard flag in a carrier, in hand.
Thoughts went back to his war,
In the sweltering, blistering, hot midday sun.
Digging the trenches or cooking the food…
Never enough to go around.
Of the mosquitoes buzzing sound…
Or of the gunfire in the distance.
He remembered the comrades he had lost,
As with a tear in his eye, he looked,
Down to his shiny Burma Star,
Not many of us left he thought,
But he was not alone, he realised,
For his family stood also tall…
Proudly watching their Dad,
As the flag swayed gently in the breeze.

I wish I was tidy.

I wish I could be tidy,
And everything was neat!
I seem to move from one spot -
To another, like the loft!
I collect far too much,
I know when I touch,
That object again, shall I keep?
Yes! And I sit in my seat…
It will wait till another time,
Instead I will write a rhyme,
Or a long list of all to do.
I will sort it, now where's my shoe!

In my little town.

In my little town
I like to walk my dog around
Just to clear my head,
With every step that I tread…
To think back over the years,
But also to look with fresh eyes and ears.
It's the best way to look at life
Smile from inside and feel 'Alive'.

MY DANCE

My tall, dark and handsome man
I am counting the days until I hold your hand.
I have waited six years to meet a man like you
There must be times you feel this way too.
I never thought you would be from another land
And what a bonus, sun, sea and sand.
Your letters have been so kind,
they really do blow my mind.
I know this could be a holiday romance
But, in my heart I feel when we get close and dance,
I look up at your face from above
And know this is an everlasting love.

Published in – The Heart Of It
(copyright Deborah Milner)

The Glitter Ball Spins Around

The Glitter ball spins around,
And we all sway to the disco sound.
The tonic suits catch the light,
As we dance on into the night.
Clonking platforms tap the floor,
The whole crowd shouts, with a roar -
As 'Get Dancing', is played once more.
Then the turntable spins around,
As the DJ plays the latest sounds.
We smile and all join in the fun,
There were even records to be won.
Then the music slows right down…
Hopeful hearts do espy,
For a partner standing nearby,
To dance around arms entwined,
Giddy at the closeness, around and around.
Hot cheeks pressing very close,
Hoping hands get a 'cheeky' grope!
Before anytime, the last song played
We wish we could have stayed,
But it was time to walk home,
With the smart boy and his pocket comb.

The dog who wouldn't walk!

The only time he wagged his tail,
And did not want to bark and wail,
Was turning around to go indoors -The dog who wouldn't walk...
Though he thought he could mutter and talk.
You see this had come about,
And that dog had no doubt,
It was the standing on his feet,
In much of the summer heat,
And also in the winter sleet,
Had made him feel his walking was done -
Now it was time to sleep in the sun.
So he would pull on the lead,
No matter how much his owner would plead!
So no more walking on the moors,
He just would stretch and sleep all day,
Except to eat and then to play.

1960s as a child.

May we return to our beginning

A life of fun, collecting marbles and winning!

Happy times playing on the streets

Looking down at our muddy knees and 'feet's'

Riding our bikes down to the park,

Meeting friends and having a lark.

Late 1960's as a child so full of fun,

Walking on stilts in the midday sun.

Bread and Jam always our treat,

Fighting with my sister, over which mat and seat!

Were our only worries we had at nine…

Now it's so different for children, further down the line.

My Garden Gnomes

My garden gnomes went on a lorry,
Moving man said he was sorry!
When missing they both went,
As I went to a radio event…
Fred and Ted, had gone walk about,
To where they were, we had our doubt?
We all liked a lady called Lee,
So we sat in her shop for tea,
Then we searched all day,
To just no array,
For they did not want to be found.
Then at the new house on the ground,
We saw there they were!
Under a great big Fir…
But where they had been -
Remains to be seen.

A New Year

A new year is about to start,
And so I wish with all my heart,
For better things to come…
May we all again feel the sun,
Smile, laugh and have fun,
Doing things we want to do.
No more fear for all too.
Wearing our blanket of protection,
I feel 2021 is the selection,
For love is all around -
Friends, family, nature all will be unwound. ♥

Love

Once hidden in the dark.

Hidden in the dark, I look at my once broken heart and see the patterns of the tiny cracks, starting to heal over.
As I move to my eyes, I see no more tears or a constant mist…
Well, only tears of joy when I see you.
As I look out of their windows, to the outside world,
I see the beautiful roses you have sent to me.
I smell their gentle scent, they have an aroma of a summer garden at dusk.
I use my hands to touch each soft silky petal,
'Slowly,' I feel each ripple and it gives my goosebumps as I touch my lips with them -
Then I hear the door open and I know you are here and I am bathed in warmth and see only sunlight.

Don't think about love.

I look at your empty cup,
And try not to think about love.
I look at the empty chair
And know you are not there.
I miss you already,
And the emptiness is steady.
But I know this will be in the past,
You will be back, if we are meant to last.

Sea of Thoughts

She sat staring out to sea,
Her mind replaying, it's not you, it's me!
Feeling alone, but also free,
Oh, on that strange day by the blue green sea.
The boat trip was like a dream,
Waves with a surf as smooth as cream.
But now the past seemed to drift away,
As she made her mind up she was going to stay.
Make a new and exciting life,
On that beautiful remote 'Isle of Fife.'

It's how the story started

The house that was not my house -

I feel I must be quiet as a mouse.

Why do I not feel a happy gaze,

I feel I am winding through a maze.

Every time I wipe my feet at that door,

After walking constant mud on the floor.

It's how the story started,

Last time we left and parted.

Now I'm back and I will try,

And not keep asking 'Why oh why'.

Mixed Poem

Roses are red
My muddled heart says stay in bed!
First you say 'Yes'
Then you say 'No'
You then say come
Then you say go.
My head says are we just friends
Or is it just that time mends?
We will have to wait and see
If it could be us, or just me.

Enclosed in.

Like a caged bird,
I can not fly.
I am so enclosed in this house,
With no way out!
The walls are imminently, closing in.
Am I here in my skin?
Help me speak…
And take me out.
Do not leave me here to wallow,
And to feel so old and sad.
Hug me and tell me it will be alright.
And that I will not be alone!
Sooth my tiredness,
As I feel you hold me tight.

Her Dating Game

She was so tired of the 'dating game'
Grumpy, too tall, but mostly too small!
Some sitting munching Cheese & Onion crisps…
Or trying to 'tear you to strips'.
Many were always arriving late
And secretly not really wanting to date.
Even trying to hide they were Wed!
Obvious they were just hoping to get you into bed!!
But sometimes when you got it right,
The date could be sheer delight.
And so you dream of meeting Mr Right,
Just not a date that gave you a fright.

Nature

Snow.

Crisp and cold,
Icy and bold.
Glistening under foot.
Feet slide in boot.
Walking in a wood…
Coat with hood.
Hands go in -
Tight stiff skin.
Snowball fights to win.
Cold with knocking knees,
Spying pretty patterns on trees.
Rosy pink cheeks
Friends to seek.
Back by a fire,
Then return to the frozen mire…
For fun riding the sled,
Till time to turn into bed.

All the flowers unite

Where waters darkly flow
And bright rainbows glow.
Full moons shine like silk
Then a valley lights like milk,
There all the flowers unite
Standing with their buds shut tight,
Bursting to open in the sunlight.
In the soil bright daisies fight
For room for their roots to grow
Where a burst of many seeds,
Like tiny dappled beads…
Scatter and again re-create,
Once more to await -
The visual magic of nature
As the scented borders call and lure.

Pigeons Fly

As they flew from their box to the sky
The pigeons reached up so very high.
Wing tips stretched up, maybe ten or so,
How do they remember where to go?
Is it by following just one…
Or do they go by the rays of the sun?
We will never really know
How homewards they no,
But it is good they don't roam,
And always find a way home.

Carl and the Carp

Carl liked to fish for Carp,
He knew the best ways being very sharp.
He had of course to go without,
If there had been a heavy drought.
There he sat and waited for hours on end,
Sorting his rigs drove him around the bend…
But all was well late at night
When he saw a wondrous sight!
A tug on his line,
Made him quickly wind,
To the bounty with all his rack,
He smiled, looked, but always put the fish back.

Trev the Rev

Trev the Rev, as we said,
Lived in the Vicarage overhead.
We used his big garden to camp,
With our sausages and beans, crouched in the damp,
Over little fires to warm our hands…
As Girl Guides we sat in our little bands.
All you could hear was 'Dib, Dib, Dob' shouts,
With here comes tea overhead from the Scouts.
He was kind and knew every tree,
And let us stay there for free.

Buttercup.

Butterflies flit and fly
Under the clear blue sky
Twisting and turning in a field of colour
Time stands still as you watch with joy
Every flutter takes you back and you enjoy
Remember as a child your love of nature
Can we stop and just don't do
Unstressed and happy everyone of us too
Pleasing yellow of buttercups shining up at you.

My Sister and I

My Sister and I,
Walked over a stile.
Into a field of green
What a sight, not often seen...
Brimstone butterflies were all around,
Flitting up high, without a sound.
In a sea of pale yellow,
We both felt so happy and mellow.
As we sat by a hedge,
On a little wooden ledge.
Buzzing all around
With their noisy sound,
The bees took over, darting in daisies
Until the sun had gone hazy
To collect the nectar for the hive,
We felt so glad to be alive.

The Lily Pad

From the deep dark water

In the depths far below,

A long plain stalk, reaches up.

Through the cold bleak times,

Trying to reach the sunlight -

Struggling to climb on its passage

Then entering the cool morning breeze,

Joining the other buds …

Until a wondrous sight appears!

A blanket of glorious red -

As the lily flowers open

In flouting synchronization

Until the sun, slowly sets.

Christmas Lights Reflections.

Christmas
lights
reflections
Is the best
sight to see.
The twinkle of
reds, yellow
and green,
Shinning down
on me.

Christmas trees
stand tall and proud
Mingling in shadows while,
Growing in shrouds…
Until a child on a cold winters day,
Picks the 'one' out,
Then it's homeward bound
Put it's root in a pot, for all to admire -
Again, out they come, entwined, then unwound.
Until at last, I gasp,
As I look up, a wonder of happiness,
Those bright Christmas lights…
Just make me so cheery
I reflect on being a child

Once a year that feeling comes,

And there is no more gloom

As they light up my heart once more.

Rock pools with Dad.

By the sea we walk with our red buckets and nets,
To dip in the crab pools before the sunsets.
With Dad on holiday, my sister and me,
We looked on so excitedly, as we sat silently.
Knelt by the gentle sea of blue,
The sun, was shining on down too.
In went our little hands,
Right down into the grainy sand.
Then out popped two little crabs,
Who made us laugh, with sideways dabs.
All the smiles and happy talk,
Collecting our pebbles and some chalk.
Such easy going childhood days,
With a lasting memory... that stays.

Into The Apple Orchard

Into the apple orchard we go…

Sweet smelling apples lay all around,

Crunching underfoot as we tread.

The sun shines down on us with intense warmth,

A little bumblebee buzzes around me,

Then in the swathes of countryside, swing apples overhead.

With my little basket, I reach…

But stop as a thud hits my head,

I reach again, but still can not stretch -

Far enough to free the rosy apple down,

Then I look down at the ground

Grabbing a long thin stick,

I start to jab and swing it around,

As I smile to see the shining apple

In my basket is not one -but three.

I had a frog

I had a frog
I placed on a log,
In my little pond.
He would hop around,
Without a sound.
But in the garden,
I looked at Marvin,
And it was sad,
One day to see he had…
When showing my daughter
Gone from the water,
And my little pet,
Was no longer wet,
His time had come,
As he lay still in the sun.

My Best Friend

You knocked on my door,
At a quarter past four,
And asked me around for tea…
You knew I lived alone and going out of my tree!
"I've just been cleaning my pond," you said,
Can you help me get some weeds, from the bed?
'Be careful,' it's very slippery here!
Just as we fell in laughing, trying to veer.
I knew I had a good friend for life,
Whenever we had trouble and strife.
As you lived next door,
For twenty years or more.
Best friends we came to be,
Happily drinking lots more tea.

A River Flows

Down where the swirling river flows,

Clearest grey, topped with off white.

Winding, spluttering and swirling around,

As tiny Minnows swim without a sound.

But under the beauty, lies a dark secret…

Laying flat on the gravel bed,

For as we are told, it fills us with fear,

That if you paddle where it gets deep,

A freshwater Leech of dark brown...

Can get to your leg and suck your blood!

Under the inviting cool waters,

So we just dip our toes in the edge,

And keep from harms way, fear pounding.

But as the river widens an amazing sight beholds,

A little bridge covered in shells over on the island,

Pearls of sunlight glimmer over the smooth shapes.

Calming our minds back to the wonders of life.

Wet Muddy Paws!

It's going to be wet muddy paws,
Every place is the same -
Wet and cold with the rain.
Out he plods, splashing about,
Then it's wet muddy paws.

Over the fields we walk.
We meet up with friends and talk.
Oh no! Into the river the dogs go,
Then it's wet muddy paws.

Back on to dry land,
We head for the car,
Pull out the towel, to no avail,
As they jump up …
And it's wet muddy paws.

Home, we drive in the warm.
Past all the dark clouds,
And in by the flickering fire,
As finally, it's no muddy paws!

The Night Storm

Woosh, sounds of the wind,
blowing in the trees.
Rustle and crackle of the leaves.
The wildlife takes cover,
Birds begin to hide,
deep in the hedgerow.
The startled fox darts for cover,
out of sight -
Into the black of night…
For the storm is coming,
Minute by minute,
like a quickening heartbeat,
you can hear it gathering speed.
Faster comes the sound,
of papers leaving the ground.
A dustbin blows over,
tin cans come crashing to the ground.
Then comes silence,

as in the still of night,
once again, no sound is heard.

The New Forest

In your yellow camper van,
We loaded up and off we ran,
Down to the New Forest, on to a site,
We had some supper then went out like a light.
A golden mist spun over the ground,
Sunlight rays and not a sound,
As morning came and horses neigh…
That came from a stunning brown 'bay',
As all in groups, the ponies came around,
Snorting as they stood very still -
I walked around the grassy hill,
And towards you gently with my head held down,
So happy you had been found…

Holding my hand flat, you touched it with your mane,
As children gathered playing a game,
Then, what a wondrous sight -
Ponies running off into the sunlight.

Out On This Moor

Out on this moor,
I walk with every step,
Filled with great happiness.

Out on this moor
There are no doors,
Just an open space
Of vast happiness.

Out on this moor,
Through the morning mist,
I see sheer beauty,
The shapes of beauty.

Out on this moor,
Wild ponies graze,
In a glistening blanket
of greys and browns.

Out on this moor,
As I walk closer my,
heart pounds, with every step,
I reach out, but eyes are wild.

Out on this moor,
Hooves stamp with a mighty sound,
As the bracken is trodden down…
And off they run, into the rising sun.

Stories

"Happy Gardening Days."

Suzie was a very good gardener, but she was lonely. Since going to Guildford College, where she learnt all her skills, she had specialized in roses and how to expertly care for them. Along with the many other beautiful flowers, in her small, but perfectly formed garden, which had taken many hours digging and planting until late in the evening. Her Dad had been a keen gardener too and she admitted, 'she did like it very neat' and not to look too much of a DIY mess.

In her tiny cottage in Surrey, there was a little pond she had dug out, with her lemon and white dog with his floppy ears, lying watching her. He was lovely company as she lived on her own and the weekends could be very long.

She often walked Teddy in the grounds of a big old house. It seemed to be empty and the course tall grass in places needed cutting. Yellow buttercups and daisies grew in a sea of yellow and white against the dark green background.

One day she thought she had seen the shadow of a young man in one of the upstairs windows, or had she?

She thought she had better get back on the public footpath and off the route where she had been picking the wild daisies, that grew tall towards the sunlight and where she would watch beautiful butterflies, flitting up to the sky with their wings glistening in the sun's rays. 'Suzie just loved nature'. It was also a wondrous scent of all the white topped wild garlic that grew freely, in the adjoining field and had often been popped into Suzie's wonderful wild vegetable stews. She had a flare for imaginative cooking as well as her gardening.

The following day while gathering cooking ingredients to make her home-made Lemon cake, at the local village shop, as she was piling them into her little wicker basket, she was drawn to an advert -

'Two mornings a week gardener wanted'

For a walled garden, experience preferred.

Apply to The Grange

Nower Lane.

She felt excitement go through her body, when she realised it was the big old house she walked in most days and where she had been picking her wild flowers a day ago!

She was very excited to be invited to the house to talk about the job and even more, she hoped, to be meeting the mysterious man at the window. She stood up when the door handle clicked and he entered the Orangery, where she was waiting a little nervously. He was taller than she had expected and he indicated for her to sit down on the elegant sofa.

"I'm John," he held out his hand to shake hers. She looked into his eyes, a little tired, she thought. He went on, "I would very much like someone to recreate a garden that surrounded a property I once owned in Costa Calida." His tanned skin, she noticed, was certainly a reflection of a man who had spent many a day in Spain. And with an air of nostalgia, he explained, "it was a walled garden full of scented roses, mainly yellow, with big blooms." She followed his gaze out of the window into the garden and realised it was the same window she had seen him looking out of before, beyond from eyes as blue as the Mediterranean itself. "Do you think you could do that Suzie?" She tried to contain her excitement at the prospect, explaining her training and experience and how much she had admired the garden on her daily walks, through the grounds. "Then the job is yours Suzie" and, with a look that she could only interpret as delight, he shook her hand adieu, and held her eyes just a fraction longer than goodbye.

While digging in the garden and adding some compost from the bag, she heard a strange sound. It sounded like a young girl quietly singing, she seemed to be playing just outside the old garden wall. Suzie popped her head outside the gate to have a look.

She saw a child around seven years old, playing with a doll with a yellow dress on as she sang to it.

"Hello, my name is Suzie," the child looked up at her and said, "My Daddy said I'm not allowed to talk to strangers," as she looked towards the house, so too did Suzie, just as John came running out. He explained to

Beth his daughter lived away in Bridgewater the next town, with his sister, since his wife died suddenly and that Beth had a tendency to wander off in the gardens. The little girl smiled and started running towards the house.

John looked at Suzie and affirmed, "I love the scent coming from that rose and what you have done". He turned to follow Beth back into the house, but as Suzie turned to go back in the gateway and finish for the day, she saw him glance back to look at her and she blushed, much to her surprise.

Suzie had been on her own for a long time. She had been with a boyfriend, who had gone to live in Australia and after trying to carry on a long-distance relationship, she found it did not work, after discovering her Skype calls had got less and less!

It broke her heart when he spoke all the time of his new great 'friend' and she knew it was over.

Pushing the bag on the shelf of the greenhouse, she stopped, bent down and felt the soft silky petals of the rose she would plant the next day and felt each ripple and it really gave Suzie goosebumps as she pictured the deep look John had given her.

It really was time to go home, so after walking up the path and waving to the garden bench, she could see John sitting at in the distance, she cycled home to feed her little dog and herself. Then after a good soak in a deep hot bubble bath, breathing in the gorgeous burst of Lemongrass and Thyme, as she daydreamed of living in The Grange and walking in the Thyme, Rosemary and sage herb garden, she decided on an early night.

Suzie was told of an open garden day at The Grange, the village shop was full of chatter about it, at the end of July. It arrived too soon as Suzie spent her days getting the rose garden full of yellow blooms ready for the big day, which was for charity.

On the open day and feeling quite proud, she had managed the hard planting and staking of the flowers, a woman in a long floaty dress with huge balloon sleeves and speaking in a loud, very well-spoken voice, keep touching John's arm as she walked around and glaring at Suzie, as she was talking to a small party about caring for the roses. Her name was Karen and she kept making rude comments and saying "Oh you mean just the new gardening girl; she has not worked here long!"

It transpired from a helper in the kitchen, that Karen had her sights pinned on John as her parents owned a large property nearby, but he had never felt any attraction towards her at all. Suzie overheard her talking as she took some coffee cups back to leave in the sink.

Suzie had always had a kind and sunny disposition and was starting to feel very sad at being spoken to in such a way. As tears pricked her eyes, that she was trying to push back, to her surprise, John walked up and stood next to her and then looked straight at Karen and said, "I think it's time you left, I have had an important telephone call and we need to close now." He then turned to Suzie and said, "Can you stay a while, I need to talk to you." As the garden cleared until the last person had gone and the main gate had been shut, he said, "I have to tell you, I have so enjoyed you coming every day and all our chats. I feel so sad when you go home.' He had been lonely before. She was lovely and he hoped they would be a couple.

As he said this and Suzie smiled, again to her surprise, he gently pulled her towards him and as he said 'May I', and gave her a soft kiss. He then turned, reached to a tray, picked up two glasses of elderberry wine and said 'Happy

Gardening Days' and he was sure they would live happily together in English garden bliss and inside Susie felt more contentment than she had felt for years. And she could not help her eyes be drawn to the yellow roses swaying in the gentle breeze, that had brought them together.

The House Warming Gift.

Not far from Pevensey Harbour there was a strange little beach house, well,

really it was a small wooden shack. The timber needed painting and it had

four uneven steps leading up to its peeling door, where many a fierce storm

had taken its toll. All around the perimeter were large pebbles.

Inside there was just a tiny kitchen with a little butler sink, a chair and a door

leading into one bedroom with nothing but a hard little bed. One insulting

comment came from a visiting Cousin, who said you wouldn't be sure if it did

not have a bed bug or two, but it was very clean!

Still Anne loved coming here, she never felt so alone when she came and

stayed with her little shaggy dog Chas, who was always very good.

All around were great big houses where the wealthy neighbours lived, but

Anne didn't mind it was hers and a getaway from her rented house where she had always felt so isolated and alone, with no doubt that anyone ever missed her when she went out of her front door.

But here in the beach shack she talked to lots of friendly people, one of them was the octogenarian lady that she passed most days. She was very interesting as she had been a writer and knew so many things about the area. A lady now of habit liking to sit in the little bakery and coffee shop every day, for her morning cup of strong coffee.

On this June day Anne had been asked to join her.

Anne smiled and walked up the pretty garden which was filled with flickering amber candles at night and sat next to the lady who on this occasion told her that her name was Pat.

'Now my dear, my life will expire one day in the future, but please don't be sad, I've had a wonderful and unbelievable life where many of my stories and books have come from, especially my travels to distant countries.

'I have something I would like to give you for your beach home, call it a 'House warming present', the obsolescence of old and no longer used technology will give you an idea what it is. I would like you to come and see it'.

Anne of course had nothing else to do! Her past relationship had ended in tears when he went trotting back to his ex and she felt a lot of her confidence had gone with him.

Obligingly, she followed Pat home.

The house was huge on the wealthy stretch of the beach, as Anne sat in the glass sun room with the sun shining, 'here my dear, if this is of any use to you' It was a beautiful vintage typewriter with pearl keys. 'I am sure you will have a story to tell, you are such a kind girl'.

'Are you sure you no longer want it?' 'No its yours, my Grandson will never use it now. Oh, I forgot to mention, he is coming to visit me this afternoon. Anne, meet Grant', and with a shy smile, she looked up at the tall, friendly man with a caring smile standing before her, 'Grant is a writer too you know', Pat added with a wink.

The Coven.

She lived in our little village and wore a long black cape. All the
children in the village were scared of her, as she kept her head down
and carried a little basket... with her hood up you could never see
her face!
They all said it was a coven, the small old stone house in Effingham.
We would peer in the small window all covered in cobwebs, sometimes
tapping on it then running away. I was sure I saw her one day, looking
over her shoulder at us, as her black cat sat on the window sill
looking out at Jill and I and a few friends we had brought along,
filling their heads with tales of witches and 'evil spells'.
I am sure one day I saw her picking herbs in her side garden and then
charging indoors when she saw us coming looking sadly at the ground.
They said she lived with another witch... but I never saw anyone else!

Then one day at the end of September, I was riding my bike and it had
been raining the night before... then it happened! I went into a skid
and came off my new red bike right outside her house. I looked down
and could see my knee bleeding and my leg felt very sore. As I looked
up the lady in the cape was looking down at me... I nearly jumped out

of my skin as she said 'Come in, I can sort that knee out for you'.
Reluctantly I could see the little wooden seat was only a couple of
feet away so limping I sat down.

As I looked around, I could see her looking around her kitchen and
gathering those herbs she had been picking in her little garden. I
gave a little shiver when she returned, but she had a pretty little
white cotton handkerchief, with some sweet-smelling herbs in it and
placed it on my knee and said that she would telephone my Dad, to pick
me up so I gave her my telephone number.

While we waited, she told me how she cared for her ill mother who
didn't leave the house. As I looked at her face, I could see worry
across it and that she was only around the same age as my Mum, maybe
30. She explained she was interested in herbs and how they healed and
really the 'White witch' title had come from this. She was very kind
and not at all frightening. I thanked her and went off with my Dad and
my buckled wheeled bicycle.

I never called her names from that day on, I smiled and waved. I also learnt not to judge people who may be a little different.

Growing Marrows.

"I'm still hungry", shouted Sonia, ''I didn't have enough for tea''. It was often the same story, Lynne did her best for her family, but she felt a little confined to the house and taken for granted!

It was as she hit her mid-forties and had gained a little too much weight around her middle, that and wanting to eat a healthier diet, that Lynne decided to take on a little allotment, well more a patch of earth at the back of a friend's garden.

Hearing the local radio station say 'there would be a competition and prize giving for the largest marrows and Sunflowers" that had really caught her interest.

Lynne gathered all the gardening books she could read on the subject and in-between all her house cleaning she went down to her little shed to read them and to start growing a few small marrow seedlings. Flowers had been easier for Lynne; she had grown them as her daughter Sonia and son Mark had grown up to their teenage years, but, 'marrows' that was an excellent challenge.

The next day Lynne acknowledged the gardening group's entry form by filling in all her details and sent it off.

Family life had been hard lately, Peter her husband, had been made redundant from the local 'Factory Warehouse,' as a line manager and was now just covering some shifts at the local supermarket's garage! Money was tight so growing your own food could be very useful too.

Lynne kept what she was doing to herself, after all it was an experiment. The day came to go to the 'little patch of ground' and sow her first row of marrows. She dug over a couple of feet, marked her line, and put them in the ground.

Back at home for teatime, it was Mark's turn, ''I need more potatoes Mum, this won't fill me up! And I've got footie practice tomorrow!'' With Lynne's usual fixed smile, she took one of the two potatoes from her plate and put it on his plate. Lynne felt sadness at not being able to do much right lately.

She went excitedly down to the veg patch, just as her old friend Ted, was leaning over his garden wall. ''Looks like you've had some bad luck there, could have been wildlife or vandals, dug them all up!''
Lynne felt greatly upset, seeing her row of carefully planted vegetables, strewn across the earth and reaching the nearby path!
"Never mind Ted", Lynne said being her usual positive self, "I have some more at home.'' ''Alright Duck,'' Ted said, "I will give you a hand, don't give up, never do that, we will make a little net and wire cage over them" … so the next day that is what they did.
As the weeks passed, they grew bigger and bigger, until Lynne was ready to enter her biggest dark green marrow, and to her delight, she won first prize!

The next night she could not wait; she mixed up all the other vegetables, courgettes, carrots chopped into a wonderful mouth-watering tomato sauce, she found the biggest roasting dish she could find and set to work.

That night as everyone crowded around the table and the 'I'm hungry' cries rang out! of course from Sonia and Mark with Peter looking on glumly, Lynne carried in the huge roasting dish with her prize marrow to the middle of the table with the 'First Prize' rosette positioned on the top.

''Now'' Lynne said, "eat up let us not waste any of my hard work!" Everyone looked at each other and smiled and no one said they were hungry again… although Lynne did think with harvest time coming and after stuffed marrows done in so many ways, the sweetcorn would make a nice change next!
Time to pop out the back door to fetch some, Lynne thought. She felt very fulfilled and appreciated now.

Debbie Milner

Printed in Great Britain
by Amazon